M000203057

INKED KINGDOM

AN UNDERWORLD KINGS ROMANCE

CARRIE ANN RYAN

INKED KINGDOM

An Underworld Kings Romance
By Carrie Ann Ryan

Inked Kingdom
An Underworld Kings Romance
By: Carrie Ann Ryan
© 2021 Carrie Ann Ryan
eBook ISBN: 978-1-63695-212-3

This book is licensed for your personal enjoyment only. This book may not be re-sold or given away to other people. If you would like to share this book with another person, please purchase an additional copy for each person or use proper retail channels to lend a copy. If you're reading this book and did not purchase it, or it was not purchased for your use only, then please return it and purchase your own copy. Thank you for respecting the hard work of this author.
All characters in this book are fiction and figments of the author's imagination.

For Jenika
Thank you for your certain hero.

"Count on Carrie Ann Ryan for emotional, sexy, character driven stories that capture your heart!" – Carly Phillips, NY Times bestselling author

"Carrie Ann Ryan's romances are my newest addiction! The emotion in her books captures me from the very beginning. The hope and healing hold me close until the end. These love stories will simply sweep you away." ~ NYT Bestselling Author Deveny Perry

"Carrie Ann Ryan writes the perfect balance of sweet and heat ensuring every story feeds the soul." - Audrey Carlan, #1 New York Times Bestselling Author

"Carrie Ann Ryan never fails to draw readers in with passion, raw sensuality, and characters that pop off the page. Any book by Carrie Ann is an absolute treat." – New York Times Bestselling Author J. Kenner

"Carrie Ann Ryan knows how to pull your heart-strings and make your pulse pound! Her wonderful Redwood Pack series will draw you in and keep you reading long into the night. I can't wait to see what comes next with the new generation, the Talons. Keep them coming, Carrie Ann!" –Lara Adrian, New York Times bestselling author of CRAVE THE NIGHT

"With snarky humor, sizzling love scenes, and brilliant, imaginative worldbuilding, The Dante's Circle series reads as if Carrie Ann Ryan peeked at my personal wish list!" – NYT Bestselling Author, Larissa Ione

"Carrie Ann Ryan writes sexy shifters in a world full of passionate happily-ever-afters." – *New York Times* Bestselling Author Vivian Arend

"Carrie Ann's books are sexy with characters you can't help but love from page one. They are heat and heart blended to perfection." *New York Times* Bestselling Author Jayne Rylon

Carrie Ann Ryan's books are wickedly funny and deliciously hot, with plenty of twists to keep you guessing. They'll keep you up all night!" USA Today Bestselling Author Cari Quinn

"Once again, Carrie Ann Ryan knocks the Dante's Circle series out of the park. The queen of hot, sexy, enthralling paranormal romance, Carrie Ann is an author not to miss!" *New York Times* bestselling Author Marie Harte

INKED KINGDOM

I fell for Sarina the moment I saw her.

When the Kingdom tore her for me, I promised revenge.

My claim was forfeit the moment she ran, but now I will follow.

I will find her.

I will earn her.

And I will burn the world if they dare touch her. Again.

CHAPTER ONE

Stone

THE FIST SLAMMED into my jaw, the crunch of flesh to bone echoing in my head. I stumbled back and tried to fight, but the person holding me back tightened their grip, my arms pinned behind me.

"Fucking take it, Stone," the man in front of me grumbled as he hooked his fist out again, this time connecting with my ribs.

I let out a shocked gasp, annoyed with myself for doing it. Eddie's eyes narrowed into slits, the glee in them familiar. Eddie loved doling out pain and seeing others fall.

The fucking bastard. The fact I'd broken just the bit that I had would egg him on, and I had been doing so well not saying a damn word. As long as I didn't make a sound, Eddie would get tired and stop.

Now he wasn't going to stop anytime soon.

Fuck.

"The King already told you what you could fucking do with your retirement, Stone. You think you're too good for us? The King *made* you. He took you from nothing. Kept a roof over your head when your own father didn't even want you. When your dear old mother left you to rot in the alley with your brother. The King kept you alive when that rat bastard of a brother finally kicked the bucket as he should have long before. Who the fuck do you think you are?"

Rage ravaged my body, threatening to overpower me and make me lose control. If I lost control, I'd die. I wouldn't be able to face Eddie and keep up with the man behind me long enough to draw in my next breath.

"I'm not a pretty boy like you, it seems," I finally answered, with a smirk of my own, and the man holding me kneed me behind my legs. I let out a curse, and Eddie grinned.

"That's a pretty boy. Look at you, pretending you're some tough shit when all you're going to do is go cry to your mother." Eddie grinned again. "Oh, you can't do that because your mom is dead. I guess that's what happens when you go against the King. You know she screamed when she died. Bent to save you, and yet it's not going to be enough. She's dead. Now you're going to join her soon. I can't wait to tell the King to send you to meet your mom. She was hot, though. Kind of miss the fact that I never got to tap that."

Fury boiled through me, and I pulled at the other man, at Rook.

His name wasn't Rook. That was his title. Eddie was the Knight. We were part of the Kingdom, its organization outside of Desolation, New York. We ran guns, booze, drugs—anything to make the King richer.

I had been born into the life, I hadn't had a choice.

I might say that I could get out, but there was no leaving it. The only person that had left had been the one person that I'd loved.

Only Sarina was gone. She had been the Princess, daughter of the former Knight, sister of the older Rook, before everything had changed.

3

Now her family was dead, and Sarina was gone, and I was alone here.

Alone in a city of crime, of terrible choices, no getting out.

Somehow I was going to leave.

I had no other choice. If I wanted to live to see my next birthday, or fuck, see the next sunrise, I needed to leave before the rest of the Kingdom put me in front of the King.

"Fuck you." I growled out the word, knowing I needed to leave. I needed to be who I needed to be and fuck everyone else.

There was no way that I could stay here. No way that I could survive if I stayed with the Kingdom, in New York, or with any attachments to the Ruin.

The Ruin was made up of the major powers of crime and unorder congregated in Desolation, New York. It connected all the bosses, the cartels, the mobs, the games, and the outsiders. Anyone who was anyone in our part of the country was connected to the Ruin.

And I needed to sever that connection if I wanted to survive.

If I wanted to have her.

I had claimed her once, and she had left. Not to

leave me, but to save herself, the one thing I hadn't been able to do on my own.

She ran from me once, from my world, from *our* world, and now I needed to find her. But the first thing I needed to do was get out of their hold.

"You really thought you could do it," Eddie said as he shook his head. He gestured behind me, and I frowned because the man holding me didn't move. No, instead, there was a sound of boots on cement and someone being dragged.

I froze, ice sliding up my veins. I looked at Jeremy.

Jeremy was the single friend I had left in the Ruin. He was a runner like me, but he tended to make poor decisions. Even worse than I did when it came to this life. I didn't do drugs. I didn't beat women. I didn't use anybody other than myself. Jeremy tried his best to emulate that but sometimes made the wrong choices.

Still, Jeremy was my only friend.

Eddie looked at me then and pulled the Glock out of his holster.

"You both thought you could leave?" He shook his head. "Guess you were wrong, weren't you?"

"I swear, I wasn't going to leave. I love the Kingdom. I love the King. I bow before him." Jeremy began to ramble, tears slid from his eyes, and I just blinked, wondering what the fuck Jeremy had done.

Because while I was going to leave, because I had to, Jeremy was supposed to wait. He had wanted to stay. He would never betray me or his King. What the fuck had he done to warrant this reaction from the Knight?

"The King sends his regards, Jeremy. Next time, don't fuck his daughter."

Jeremy let out a scream, and then there was nothing, just the sound of a gunshot echoing between my ears and my stomach falling out.

This couldn't be happening. Jeremy couldn't be dead. The Knight hadn't just killed a man in cold blood in front of me. But of course he had. They'd done it before. And if I wasn't careful, they'd do it again and again until there was no hope.

No salvation.

Jeremy fell, the single perfect precision hit right in the middle of his forehead. Eddie sighed and put the gun back in his holster.

"We're going to have to get the cleaner in here to clean this up," he growled. "Do you want to use ours or someone else's?"

"Call Arlo." Rook chuffed behind me. "That

way, our guy doesn't have to get his hands dirty. Arlo will be good at it."

Ice crawled all over me. Arlo was the cleaner for higher-ups in the Ruin. Nobody knew exactly what he did, but as Arlo worked for the Petrov Bratva. He was a big mean son of a bitch.

Nobody messed with him, and if Arlo was coming here to clean up the mess Jeremy made, he was here to clean me up too.

I swallowed hard, looked at my dead friend, and I wondered how the fuck I got here.

I was such an idiot.

I needed to get out of here. I needed to get out of the life that I had no choice in until now.

I couldn't even feel remorse for the friend that was dead. I didn't have time or the luxury to *feel*. Everything was numb. Hollow. Unending.

Jeremy was dead. And he had cried.

And I was next.

"I think the King wants to do this personally for you, boy," Eddie said as he shook his head. "I'm not going to waste a bullet on you."

Then Eddie moved forward and snapped out his wrist. The taser hit me right in the chest, sending electric shocks down my body. I hadn't even realized that the Rook had let me go, was laughing behind me. I fell to my knees, and then the taser was gone, and they were kicking. Steel-toed boots hitting my side, my ribs. Something cracked and I coughed up blood. And then there was a fist to my temple, and there was nothing.

"Wake up, dumb ass. Open those eyes."

I looked up into the dark eyes of the man above me and figured maybe this was how I was going to die. Maybe the King didn't want anything to do with me after all.

"Come on, before they take you to the hub, the Ruin doesn't need to see your dead body. And neither do I."

"Arlo?" I asked as I coughed.

Arlo looked down at the blood that I had sprayed on his chest and rolled his eyes. "Thanks for that. Come on, let's get you out of here."

"What the fuck?"

"You want out? I got you a car. No questions."

"But how? Why?"

"See, those are questions. And I don't want fucking questions."

"I don't understand."

"You don't need to understand. Just get the fuck out of here, Stone. You want to survive? Leave."

"But what about you?"

"There are different ways to survive, Stone. You know that better than anyone else." He tossed the keys at me, and I caught them with my left hand, my right one still aching from when Eddie had stomped on it.

"What are you going to tell them?"

"Again with the questions. It's like you want to be killed."

He shook his head and walked off without saying another word, as if speaking to me had been too much for him in the first place.

I looked over at the small nondescript sedan in front of me and wondered what the fuck was going on. My head ached, and I had a feeling I might have a concussion, but I ignored it.

I got in the car, started the engine, and wondered if I was trusting the wrong person. After all, I had been trusting the wrong people my entire life. What was one more wrong choice?

I needed to go, needed to find my home. The only home that I could think of was the one who had left me, the one who had needed to run, the one I hadn't gone after.

But there was no time like the present.

My only friend was dead, taken away when I was out cold, and I hadn't even had time to mourn or wonder what I could have done.

My family was long gone, taken from me before I'd had the strength to fight back to try to save them.

All that would be left for me at the Ruin were the death and destruction of whatever the King declared.

So I started the engine and I pulled away, wondering what the fuck Arlo was thinking and how the fuck I was going to repay him.

In the end, it didn't matter because I was looking for her.

For Sarina.

My life was forfeit.

The claim I once had on her long gone.

My past lay in ruins, but she was the one for me.

She would be my salvation.

Or my ending.

CHAPTER TWO

Sarina

I TOSSED the recycling in the dumpster and shook my head. Well, standing in an alley surrounded by dumpsters and trash was at least better than my former life. It wasn't glamorous, but it was mine.

My back ached, my feet hurt, but to me, that just meant an excellent job for the day. I still had another shift at the bar later, but for now, being a barista at Café Taboo paid some of my bills.

That's why I worked as a bartender at Ink on Tap, the gay bar down the street that my best friend owned, in the evenings.

I didn't have a life, but that was fine. Who needed a life when you were working two full-time jobs and sleeping when you could? I didn't need a life outside of that.

At least, that's what I told myself.

After all, I had lived dangerously and a little more high-octane when I had been in high school. I didn't need anything more than this.

I rolled my shoulders and turned towards the other side of the alley to get back into the café and finish my shift. I tripped over a rock, my whole body turning to ice as I looked at the person in front of me.

It was a ghost. It had to be a ghost because he couldn't be there.

After all this time, that couldn't be Stone Anderson standing in front of me. The one person I had left, the one person that had taken everything from me.

Or rather, perhaps I had taken everything from him.

I had given him myself, my innocence, my heart, my future, and he had thrown it away because he chose his family over me.

He had chosen everything over me.

"Stone," I whispered, my voice cracking.

"You remembered me."

I blinked at him, my hands shaking. "What happened to your face?" I asked, wondering why that was the first thing that came out of my mouth. Of course, it couldn't be helped. He looked horrible.

Perhaps beneath the split lip, black eye, and swollen cheekbone, there was still that gorgeous ruggedness that was Stone, but I could barely see it. No, instead, all I could notice were the imperfections, the signs that perhaps he hadn't left the life like he had promised me he would.

He had stayed behind when I left, and whatever had wrapped its hands around his neck had taken more from him that I could comprehend.

"Sarina," he whispered, his voice a growl. It did things to me, just like it always had. That was the problem with Stone.

No matter what I did, I couldn't think when he was around. He made me lose all sense, lose all reality.

Because he was supposed to be my everything. My salvation. My one true everything.

And then he had chosen the Kingdom.

Chosen the place that had killed my father. Killed my brother. Killed everything.

Chosen the place that had wanted me. Not for who I was, but what I could do for them.

They had wanted my body, my soul. They had wanted everything other than who I was and what choices I could make.

Stone had chosen them.

How was I supposed to look at the man in front of me and want anything other than to run?

So I did. I left the alley. I turned on my heel, and I ran.

My feet dug into the gravel, and I ignored the blisters on my heels. I ignored Stone's shout.

I ignored him.

I'd have to call Hailey later and let her know why I had left in a hurry, but she would understand. She had to. She and all of her family always understood what was going on. It was as if they had a sixth sense. They would understand why I had to leave. They might not know every detail, they knew enough to understand my running. At least for the day, and if Stone wouldn't walk away, perhaps forever.

I had been hiding in Denver for four years, but maybe this would be my last moment. Maybe I would have to fully leave and never come back. Never return to the place that I had called home for so long.

I ran down the block, and nobody paid me any mind.

They were all focusing on their own lives, their own problems. Nobody cared about the woman in the apron running for her life.

I had left my purse behind, everything. The only thing I had was my phone, and whatever wits I had left.

Because if Stone was here, the Kingdom couldn't be far behind.

And I needed to be safe.

I couldn't be near them.

Because if the Kingdom found me, I would be dead. My life would be forfeit, as would everything else I had ever thought I could possibly have.

Because once the Kingdom had you, there was no leaving. The King had wanted me for his Queen, even at a barely legal age.

He had seen what Stone had, and had wanted me. His own Queen had died only six months prior, and everyone said it had just been an accident. We all knew that was a lie. The old Queen, Gwen, had been the Guinevere to her Arthur and had found her own Lancelot. She had cheated on the King, fallen in love with the wrong man. With the one man, she couldn't have and he hadn't been ruthless enough to save them.

She died at the hands of her own King, of her husband.

And the King wanted me.

And when I said no, he killed my brother, his Rook.

And when my father, his Knight, had fought for me, he killed him too.

Their blood still stained my palms; I could see them in my dreams, hear their screams. In the end, there was nothing I could do.

I had run. I hadn't run far enough, it seemed.

It was never going to be far enough.

Stone had found me. And soon, the new Rook and the new Knight would as well.

Stone was their runner, their tracker.

And the others would follow, and I would die. Because I would die before I fell before the King as a supplicant.

Before I became his bride.

Before I filled his bed.

I would die.

I pounded on the backdoor to Ink on Tap, praying that Rebel could hear me.

"What the fuck, Sarina?" Rebel asked as he pulled open the door. He was shirtless and in sweats and looked like I had just woken him up. Maybe I had. It was still early enough in the day that he was probably sleeping upstairs in the apartment that he owned rather than working on opening up the bar. Of course, nobody would be here other than him for the next hour or so, but it didn't matter. I needed to find a place to be safe. I needed to be safe.

"Can I come in?" I asked, my whole body shaking.

Rebel gave one look at me, tugged me in by my apron, and slammed the door behind me, locking it. "What's wrong? Are they after you?"

Rebel had left the Kingdom long before I had. He had dropped out of high school and ran before they could destroy his soul and his heart. That was over fifteen years ago, and now he owned Ink on Tap, the prominent gay bar for the area, the one that was inclusive, a safe house, and a safe place.

It was my salvation, the one place I could be myself.

The one place Rebel could be his self.

And I was going to have to leave it.

"Stone's here," I blurted.

Rebel cursed under his breath. "Is he alone? How did he find you?"

"I think he's always known where I was. Of course, he would."

"Fuck. Okay, we can get you some new identification, get you out of here."

"I left my purse and everything behind. I'm such an idiot. All I have is my phone."

"Okay, we'll get you out of here. I know somebody up in Wyoming. They can keep you safe."

"Really? Is that going to be the best I can do? Running for the rest of my life?"

"I don't know what else we're supposed to do, babe. I'll go with you. So you're not alone."

"You can't give up everything."

"I would. You know I would. My family's long dead and the King won't even remember who I am. After all, he didn't know me as Rebel."

I nodded and sighed. "Okay. I guess I'll leave? I don't know. I don't know what I'm supposed to do."

Rebel opened his mouth to speak and then frowned, pulling out his phone. "Well. It seems that Stone found you. Fuck. Okay, we'll get you out another way. Unless they have us surrounded." He let out a breath. "It's been so long since I've done this. I'm rusty."

Stone's voice came through the doorbell camera alert. "Sarina? I'm alone. I left. I promise you. I left."

Rebel and I both froze, my palms damp, bile filling my throat. "Did he say he *left*?"

"That's what he says. Fuck, it looks like somebody did a number on him." Rebel met my gaze. "Sarina, babe. Stone would never have hurt you. You know that. He might have stayed to protect his brother, but he always promised that he would never hurt you."

"Why are you throwing that back in my face?" I asked, my laugh hollow. "He did hurt me. Just not in the way that he might think."

"Of course he did. He's a man. He's a dumbass. He stayed in the Kingdom to protect his brother, but he's out there, looking pretty hurt, and I don't know, something doesn't feel right about this."

Tension slid up my shoulders again. "What do you mean?"

"There's nobody on my surveillance, Sarina." He showed me his phone, at the eight cameras and their feeds. "Not a single thing. And none of my contacts have warned me that any of the Kingdom's coming here. I'll reach out if you want to see what's going on with Stone, but this doesn't feel like a setup."

"Isn't that going to be the last thing that anybody says before they find out it was a setup?"

"Maybe. But come on, let's go see what Stone wants. I'll protect you."

"I'm not going to have you hurt because of me."

"It would never be because of you. You know that."

"Rebel, we left."

"And maybe Stone did too."

I swallowed hard and rolled my shoulders back. "Fine, he's never going to go away. It always seems like he can find me. I'll see what he wants, tell him to go, but you stay safe. I don't want him to see you."

"Sarina."

"What? Let me protect you for once. Maybe it's my turn. I shouldn't have come here. I put you right in the thick of things all over again."

"I'm here to protect you. Remember that."

"No, we protect each other." I kissed him hard on the mouth, and he rolled his eyes before he followed me towards the backdoor.

"Stay out of sight."

"Fine, but let me put on shoes. I'm not going to fight off a team while I'm barefoot and shirtless."

"If anyone could do it, it would be you," I teased, trying to lighten the tension.

"Sarina," Stone said again, through the doorbell camera. Rebel had the camera set up to hear what Stone was saying outside, and that was the only reason I felt somewhat like I could have control here. It took me forever to find my control, my own life.

I opened the door partway, the glass partitioning it off. It was bulletproof glass, and there was no way Stone could make it through. At least, that's what I told myself.

"Sarina. You ran."

"Of course I ran. What are you doing here, Stone? I'm not going back."

"I'm not going back either. I'm free." He shrugged, then winced, pressing his hand to his side.

"Stone." I reached up, almost getting to the door to help him, then realized what I was doing.

He wasn't going to get me this way. Nobody was going to make me feel like an idiot. "I'm fine. Just need to heal. It was a goodbye present from Eddie and the others on my way out."

"You're gone then. You just left."

"There was no just about it, but I'm out. I'm not going back." He let out a shaky breath. "I should've left long ago. I was a fucking idiot. But I needed to stay for Phoenix."

"I'm sorry about your brother." I swallowed hard. "I heard about what happened."

"Sorry about a lot of things."

Phoenix had been Stone's older brother and had died in a shootout with a rival gang. I didn't know the details, only that Phoenix was dead, and the sole reason that Stone had stayed was gone. And yet, Stone hadn't come. I had waited foolishly, as if expecting him to show up and for us to pretend that nothing had changed between us and that he had finally had a reason to stay.

In the two years since Phoenix's death Stone hadn't contacted me, hadn't shown, and that had been the final nail in the coffin of whatever dreams I had once had.

I left the Kingdom because there was only death of my soul and my body back for me with the King. I had left, with a promise from Stone that he would come for me.

And then a single note saying he couldn't because Phoenix needed him had shattered everything. Had torn away the fragile bonds of whatever promises we had made to one another.

With the death of Phoenix shocking around our underworld, I had thought maybe I had a chance. Maybe he would come back.

He hadn't. Stone hadn't come.

And so, these past two years, I had found a way to be myself, the person that I was.

Stone hadn't come for me. I had come for myself.

"I came for you; you don't have to do anything.

I'm going to stay for a while. Figure out who I need to be. But Sarina? I'm back. I'm here."

I looked at him then, looked at the man I had once loved, and I could see the parts that I had loved before, the parts that I had been connected to, but he wasn't him. I loved Stone Anderson. I had given everything to him, and he had stayed to protect his family, and while I understood that, I needed to defend myself. For once, I needed to do something for myself.

"I'm glad that you're out. But I'm not the same person. I'm not the girl that needed your help to get away from the King. I'm not the girl who watched her father and her brother die. You're free, but I've been free longer. Be safe, Stone. But I'm not yours anymore. And maybe I never was." I raised my chin, then closed the door in his face, locked it, and ignored Rebel's look. Instead, I fell to my knees, my hands ice against the cold metal steel of the door, and let the tears fall.

I had loved Stone before.

And perhaps part of me always would.

He was my past, not my present.

And if I wanted to survive, I couldn't let him be my future.

CHAPTER THREE

Stone

THANKS TO ARLO'S INTERVENTION, I had
been in Colorado and away from the Ruin and the
Kingdom for four weeks now. Four weeks of me
trying to figure out what the fuck I was going to do.

Sarina hadn't wanted anything to do with me,
and frankly, I didn't blame her. I had shown up out
of the blue, not knowing what the hell I wanted, and
she hadn't wanted me. Had practically shoved me
out of the way. And I get it. She walked away, and I
probably would've done the same in her case.

I missed her, damn it. Of course, I had missed

her when she left before, when she had gotten out and taken the step before I had. She was far stronger than I was, far stronger than I would ever be.

Not that she would let me tell her that. No, she wanted nothing to do with me, and while I was a bastard, an asshole, I wasn't about to force her into spending time with me. So that meant I had to stay away. At least until I found some form of steadiness.

I didn't go into Taboo or Ink on Tap. Those were the two places that I knew for sure that she worked.

In the past four years, she seemed to have found her place, a set of friends, maybe even a family here.

And I wasn't part of that.

Maybe I didn't need to be part of that. Hell, I wanted to be part of that. She was my goddamn forever, and I just wished somehow she would let that happen. She would fall for me again and not want to let go.

Only, if I pushed, if I crowded in, she'd hate me more than she already did. And considering I knew she despised seeing me, that was saying something.

"You ready to go, Stone?" I shook myself out of my funk and looked up at Luc, my boss.

I had been out of a job, in need of funds, and a new way to start my life.

In a past life, I had once considered becoming an

electrician. I was good at it and can usually rig up anything around me that was needed.

That was what the King had used me for when I wasn't a runner.

So I used the skills I had honed in the business to find a job here.

Now I worked at Montgomery Inc. and was working my ass off.

When I wasn't helping Luc with setting up the electric, I was lifting and hammering and sawing, doing whatever else I needed to do for the company.

An entire family owned and operated this place. It was nice seeing how one member of the family was the architect, the other the lead contractor, and one even a plumber. Luc was the electrician. He had married into the family; his wife Meghan was the lead landscape architect. They built homes and some commercial buildings, but whatever contract they got, they seemed to put their all in, always to code and worked with high-end materials.

They were the real deal, completely the opposite of what I used to do.

I felt like maybe I could find a home here, not that I thought I'd ever actually be able to stay. No, eventually, I'd have to go. Because I knew the King wouldn't let me stay for long. Maybe it was a good thing that Sarina was gone then. That she wanted nothing to do with me, because when the King found me, when he sent his men after the runner they had lost, if he even cared that much, they would find her too, and I would never let anything happen to her.

I was down on the ground, my hands covered in dirt as I lifted a box for Luc, when I heard a familiar voice. A voice that broke me.

I stiffened, even as Luc grinned widely on the other side of me.

"Hey man, we're going to take a break."

I cleared my throat and looked up at the dark-skinned man. "Excuse me?"

"My wife's here."

"Oh."

I stood up next to Luc and wiped my hands on my jeans. "I've met Meghan."

"Yeah, she's pretty great, isn't she?"

Only it wasn't Meghan I was looking at. Yes, Meghan, with her dark hair and bright blue eyes was gorgeous, but she only had eyes for Luc, just like I only had eyes for the girl next to her.

Sarina stood there, her hair piled on the top of her head, her hazel eyes wide as she looked at me.

Whatever color had been in her face from her

laughter earlier was gone. Instead, it leeched from her skin as she stared at me as if she had seen a ghost.

Maybe she had.

I wasn't supposed to be here. I had done my best to stay away. Why the hell was she here?

Luc cleared his throat and looked at me. "I know you're running. We all do. I guess you know Sarina?"

"From a lifetime ago."

When we had been young, foolish, and thought we could take on the world. But in the end, we hadn't been able to do anything. We hadn't been able to save ourselves.

"You know, I almost made a mistake before by leaving and not fighting. You might be trying to figure out who you are, but if you think she's worth it, apologize. Make sure she knows she's the center of your universe. And don't fuck it up."

I looked up at the other man and frowned. "You can tell all that from a look?"

"You can tell a lot of things when you've been there before."

Luc shrugged, set down his equipment, then walked over to his wife. "Hey there, baby."

"Hey there, baby, right back."

They kissed each other like they weren't on their worksite, as if they hadn't been married for years.

29

"What'd you bring me?"

"Hailey was busy today, a conference downtown had heard about Taboo, and now she's stressed out. She sent Sarina here with our lunches, and I said I would help."

"It's nice to meet you, Sarina," Luc said as he held up his hand. Sarina smiled, but it didn't reach her eyes. After all, she was looking at me, then she shook her head, smiled for real, and took Luc's hand.

"It's nice to meet you. Hailey always talks so well about the family. I'm glad I could finally come out here."

"I'm glad you could too." Luc swung his arm around Meghan's shoulders. "Are you going to join us for lunch?"

"Oh, I should go back. Hailey needs me."

"Okay then, just let me know what you need. I'm going to go take my wife to neck around the side."

"Luc!" Meghan laughed, but she didn't counter that. Instead, she followed him, leaving Sarina and me alone.

"You're here," she whispered.

"Yeah. I've been working here for a bit." I cleared my throat. "I didn't know you'd be here. I know you said you wanted space, and I figured I'd do the one thing I should've done a long time ago and fucking listen to you."

She shook her head and looked down at the baskets around her. "I just brought lunch for the crew. Hailey does that every once in a while. Her bakery is right next to Montgomery Ink. The two families own the business, and they're all close."

"That's cool. Luc was telling me a little bit about it."

"So, you're an electrician now?" she asked as she stared at me.

"I always have been. I didn't do it for the right things."

"No, I guess you didn't."

I shuddered, pushing away thoughts of what I'd been forced to do in the past, because I wasn't that person anymore, at least, that's what I told myself.

"Anyway, I'll leave you be. If that's what you want."

"I don't know what I want, Stone. How are you here?"

"I don't know. I didn't expect you."

"Well, to say that I didn't expect you would be an understatement."

"I'm sorry. For taking up your space. For being here. But I missed you, Sarina."

"It's been years, Stone. I already told you we're not the same people."

"You're right. We aren't. I'd still like to get to know you."

"Really?" she asked, and I could tell she didn't believe me.

"I do. I want to get to know you. I'm here for the long haul, Sarina." As long as they didn't find me. But neither one of us needed to say that.

"I left all that behind me. I don't know if I'm ready to see it again."

"I'm not that person. I left. I should've left a long time ago, but I never crossed *that* line. I was never that guy."

We both knew what I was talking about; there was no need to say the words aloud.

"I was so afraid that you'd be pushed into it. I never thought you'd willingly take that step."

"Sarina," I whispered.

"I'm just so afraid. What if you wake up and realize that you miss that life?"

"No," I said vehemently. "I'm not that guy. I left because I needed to, because I wanted to. Because I missed you."

"Don't put that all on me. Don't say that you left only for me."

"I didn't. I left because I wanted to, because I needed my life back. I stayed because of my brother, and that was wrong, but he's gone. They all are. I don't want to be part of that life anymore."

"That life is long behind me, Stone."

"Good. Then let's start over."

I held up my hand. "Hi, I'm Stone."

She looked up at me, then down at my hand, her body shaking slightly as she sucked in a breath.

"Stone," she whispered. Then she let out a breath, met my gaze, and slid her hand into mine. "I'm Sarina."

"Sarina," I whispered, relief hitting me like a two-by-four.

"I'm scared," she said, with a hollow laugh. "What if you leave again? What if I have to leave?"

"I'm not going to let anything happen to you, Sarina."

"We both know you can't promise that."

"I'll try my damned best. But we're going to start over, remember? I'm just Stone. You're just Sarina."

She looked at me then and shook her head. "I don't think there's anything *just* about that. But we can start over. Because walking away from you hurt, it killed me, and I don't think I'm strong enough to do it again." And so we stood there, as others milled

33

about, and I stared at the woman that I loved, the girl that had walked away, and the woman she had become.

I had to hope this wasn't a dream, that this wasn't going to fall around me.

I knew better.

I had always known better.

I just hoped it wasn't too late.

CHAPTER FOUR

Sarina

MY FEET HURT AGAIN, but this time I still had a slight bounce to my step.

I couldn't help it. It had been a week since I had seen Stone at the job site, since I had told myself that I wasn't making a mistake.

And I wasn't making a mistake. Because I had already made one before, by pushing him away. He had been hurting, had been in pain, and I had pushed him away to protect myself.

I shouldn't have done that. Yes, I was scared. Yes,

seeing Stone had brought back memories of pain, agony, and shame.

He had always treated me well. He had always treated me like I was cherished.

He hadn't forced me to stay behind for him. He had watched me go, had stood back to make sure I was safe.

That's what I had to remind myself.

Yes, he had stayed, no, he hadn't come after me until I felt like it was too late, but he hadn't blocked me in.

"You feeling okay?" Rebel asked me from the other side of the bar, and I smiled at him, this time knowing it reached my eyes.

"I am, ready for the night to be over though, no offense."

He just grinned at me. "Oh, no, because your honey bun is coming to stay with you for the evening. I wouldn't want to stay either."

"Rebel," I said as I blushed.

"Honeybun?" Jeremiah, one of my regulars, asked as I handed him his beer.

"It's nothing," I grumbled, glaring at Rebel. "Stop it."

"Stop what?"

Rebel beamed and leaned forward towards Jeremiah. The two had been having a serious flirt for the past couple of months, and I wish they would just ask each other out already. However, fate was a tricky mistress, and they were taking more time.

"Her old boyfriend is back in town."

"Well, if you broke up with him, it must have been for a reason," Jeremiah said. "We don't want you hurt."

My heart swelled, and I could see it did for Rebel too from the look in his eyes. "He didn't hurt me. I had to leave a situation, and he couldn't come with me."

It wasn't exactly true because he *had* hurt me because he stayed away for so long. Only that hurt was also on me.

It wasn't all his fault, nor was it all mine. Sometimes I had to remember that it was the King's fault, the Kingdom, and the Ruin.

Those who had sent us to a life that we couldn't escape. They were who had hurt us both.

I wasn't afraid of Stone. I never had been. I was afraid of what he had represented, what had almost swallowed us both.

That wasn't the case anymore. I wasn't that person anymore. I had to hope that Stone wasn't that person either.

"Anyway, her ex is back in town, and he makes her smile like that, so I'm calling it a good thing."

I blinked and looked over at Rebel. "Really?"

"Of course. I'd say he's your lobster, but we know that lobsters don't mate for life," Rebel joked.

I rolled my eyes. "Please stop telling me random crustacean facts."

"I'd like to know random crustacean facts," Jeremiah said, his gaze only for Rebel. I looked between the two of them and held back a smile. If crustacean facts and trivia were what was going to bring these two together, I wasn't going to stand in their way.

I cleared my throat. "I'm going to go clean up on the other end, and then I'm heading out. Are you two okay?"

"I think we're just fine," Jeremiah answered, and Rebel rolled his eyes.

"You think that line is going to work?"

"I think I have a few more," Jeremiah drawled when I rolled my eyes. I grabbed my bag from underneath the bar, and headed towards the other end.

I'd have to wear my cross-body bag for the rest of the evening, but that was fine. I didn't want to interrupt them again accidentally. Not when things might be working out.

"Hey," Stone whispered from my side, and I let

out a breath, my stomach tightening. I had known he was there, of course. The hairs on the back of my neck had stood on end, and I always knew he was there.

There was something about him. Something that hurt and ached and made me want to give in.

That was Stone. That was always Stone.

"Hi," I said as I looked up at him, at his deep green eyes, the way his dark hair fell over his face.

He needed to shave, and I liked it. That slight stubble that I knew would scrape rough against the inside of my thighs.

I blushed, wondering where the hell that thought had come from, and from the way that Stone's eyes darkened, he must've guessed where my thoughts had gone.

"When are you through tonight?" he asked, his voice a low growl.

"She's done now," Rebel said, not tearing his gaze from Jeremiah's.

I swallowed hard. "Apparently, I'm done now."

"Good, I'll walk you home?"

"Oh. Sure." Disappointment slid through me. In the week since we had reintroduced ourselves to one another, pretending the past hadn't existed even while it wrapped its claws around our throats, we had gone for coffee, for food, but we hadn't kissed. Hadn't done anything.

Had he wanted to start over completely by just being friends? Or was it something more? Was he just taking it slow?

I wasn't sure, but I couldn't read him, and it killed me.

Because I wanted to know, I needed to know.

I was just afraid if I asked, the answer would hurt.

Just like always, everything hurt when it came to Stone and the Kingdom.

"I have my bag, so I'm ready to go."

"Good. Come on, let's take you home."

I walked out from the side of the bar, waved at Rebel and Jeremiah, who weren't even looking at me, and found myself holding Stone's hand. His palms were rough, calloused, as if he worked hard with his hands, and I couldn't help but imagine his hands on me.

Why the hell did I feel so freaking horny? I had had sex before, mostly with myself, but it counted.

Why was it that every time I was around Stone I swooned and couldn't focus? Why was I always wet when he was around?

There was something wrong with me.

"Where are your thoughts going?" he asked as we walked down the street towards the small set of apartments where I lived. It was ridiculously priced in downtown Denver. However, I was subletting from a woman who wasn't charging too much. I wasn't sure why, and I wasn't going to ask questions, but everything was legal according to Rebel, so I would focus on that.

"What?" I asked.

Stone met my gaze, shook his head. "You're in your head, and I don't know why."

"I think you can guess why," I muttered as we walked up the stairs towards my fourth-floor apartment.

"Okay, so you're working two jobs then?" he asked as I let him inside, feeling as if the space was far too small with him around. He was wide, all muscle, and he filled any room he was in. But right then, it felt like it was more as if I couldn't breathe when he was around. Or maybe I could never breathe when he was around.

"Yes, between both jobs, seven days a week and far too many hours, but they're good to me, and I'm saving up."

"This apartment can't be cheap," he said as he looked around the fully furnished sublet apartment.

There were light colors, a modern kitchen, and a small sofa. My bed was in the corner, as it was a studio and not much square footage, but it was enough for me—more than I ever had growing up. Oh, my father had had a decent home before the Kingdom had enveloped us, but then we had moved into the compound, and I had only been given what they allowed me to have, what the King had bestowed upon us.

Because I wouldn't give him what he wanted, it wasn't enough.

"The price isn't that much. It's a sublet. And I think just good luck."

"It's great. I'm renting a hole in the wall in Aurora, and I'm pretty sure that the rats are bigger than I am, but it works."

I frowned. "I'm sorry. Did you sign a lease? We can find you something better."

"It's week-to-week, which is why it's such a shitty place. I was just afraid at first that I'd have to leave quickly, and I didn't want to sign anything. You know?"

"I do, because you're under the radar, just like I am."

"I hate that we are. I hate that he probably knows exactly where I am."

"I know he knows where I am," I said as I shrugged, setting my bag down. "He always knows. We can pretend and change our names, get a fake Social Security card, and go about all the normal ways to hide, but he'd always find us."

"That's why you never changed your name."

"I changed my last name, but there wasn't a point. He always knows where we are because if he can't find us, he has connections with the Ruin, and they can find anybody."

"There's no hiding unless you're dead."

I hadn't meant to say that, and with the storms in Stone's eyes, he didn't like to hear it. "I'm so fucking sorry."

"There's nothing to be sorry about," I said, shaking my head. "You didn't do anything wrong.

"Then why do I feel like I did something wrong?"

"Now that I think about it, you stayed to protect your brother. You survived because that was the situation we were in. I only got out because you found a way for me. And I think I hated myself more than you for you not being able to come with me."

"Sarina," he whispered as he moved forward, his hands cupped my face, and I let out a breath, the warmth of his skin on mine almost too much.

"I hated myself for leaving you behind. For not being strong enough to stay to fight for us. I know you had to stay. I know there wasn't another choice. I think, though, I hated you more than I wanted to when you couldn't come with me later. When your brother was gone, and there was nothing else."

"He chained me in the basement," he muttered, and I froze.

"What?"

He let me go then and began to pace, and I felt the coolness of lack of his touch.

"He chained me in the basement when my brother died. Beat me, did...well, things. I don't want to go into detail because I don't want to think about it. They were training the new Rook, the new Knight, and I was just the runner. They wanted me to kill this kid, this fucking kid, so that I could take over the Rook position, and I wouldn't." Stone met my gaze. "I wouldn't. And when they killed my brother, there was nothing else for me. I tried to leave, and they wouldn't let it happen. I stayed for as long as I was forced to, and then there was nothing else for me."

"Stone," I whispered.

"A friend helped me out, though I don't think he is actually a friend. An ally that I hadn't realized was an ally until it was almost too late to. He got me a car, helped me get out while I was thinking about just taking the bus to get here to you."

"Because you knew where I was," I whispered, my hands shaking.

"Of course I did. I always knew where you were, because I needed to make sure you were safe. That's why I stayed. Well, part of it. Because I needed to make sure you were safe."

Tears slid down my cheeks, and he cursed under his breath. "Stop it. I wasn't blaming you."

"I know. But damn it, Stone, why did we lose so much time?"

"We don't have to lose any more."

And then his mouth was on me, and I was lost. He tasted of coffee and Stone. I moaned into him, craving him. He was the drug, and I was the addict, and it had been too long since my last hit.

An eternity since my last hit.

I slid my hands up his back, digging my nails into his shirt, and he groaned into me, pinning me against the wall. I hadn't even realized that he had backed me up next to the front door until I was there and I groaned, arching against him. My nipples were hard, pressing against his chest, and he smiled against me. "You taste so fucking good.

Like a memory, sin, and a promise all rolled up into one."

"I could say the same of you. I missed this, Stone. I missed you."

"It's only been you," he whispered, and my eyes went wide.

"What?"

"Since you left, it's only been you."

I swallowed hard. "I waited too. I didn't realize I was doing it, but I waited."

He groaned, his thick cock pressed against my belly. "Fuck. I'm not going to last long."

"Then this first time, we don't have to last. I just need you."

"Deal."

And then he was kissing me again, pulling up my shirt. I tugged at him, ripping at the bottom of his shirt until he pulled back, shrugged off his jacket, and remove the shirt over the top of his head. He was all ink and long lines of muscle. My hands ran over the scar on his chest, the other on his hip, another on his bicep, and he cursed under his breath.

"The only scars I have are the ones of my own making. Ignore the rest."

"Only if you ignore them too."

And I tugged off my shirt, leaving me in my bra, and his fingers went to the scar between my breasts.

"I'll kill him for you."

"No. He's nothing right now. Don't let him in here."

The King didn't matter right now. He couldn't. I couldn't let him be part of this.

I may wear the King's scar on my flesh, but I wasn't his Queen. Wasn't his anything.

Stone growled, and then he kissed me again, and I was lost.

I tugged on his pants, and we each toed out of our shoes, stripping each other gently. We were still standing, my back pressed against the cool wall.

"I need to be inside you," he grumbled as I reached between us, gripping his cock. He was wide, long, and I couldn't touch my fingers as I wrapped around him.

"Were you always this big?" I asked, looking down.

He grinned. "It looks like I'm going to have to refresh your memory." And then he reached down, lifting me by my thighs, and speared into me.

I was wet, soaking for him, and he slid right in with ease.

I looked at him, my breath coming in pants as I

47

looked down between us, at the way that we connected, his cock deep inside my pussy.

"Stone."

"Fuck, I didn't mean to go so fast, but I slid right in."

"Because I'm always wet around you," I said as I clenched my inner walls. His eyes crossed, and he groaned, kissing me again. And then I wrapped my legs around his waist and urged him.

"Please. Fuck me. We'll make love later, but now I just need you to fuck me."

"Deal." Then he moved, sliding deep inside of me. He slammed me into the wall over and over again, and I arched for him, meeting him thrust for thrust. I'd be bruised later, but then again, as my fingers clawed down his back, he'd carry my mark as well.

And that's all I wanted, for him to carry my mark on his flesh, his soul, just like he had branded me long ago.

He flipped his thumb between us, over my clit, and I met his gaze. My mouth parted, and I came. It was a rush, passion and promise and heat all at once as my cunt clamped around his dick, my entire body breaking out into goosebumps as I came, my head thrown back, my body in need.

Stone bit down on my shoulder, grunting as he followed, filling me as if the both of us hadn't been able to hold back. It was hard, rough, and it was perfect.

It was only then that I looked down and realized he hadn't used a condom.

Stone was the only person I had ever had sex with, and if he was telling the truth, and I had to hope he was, I was the only person for him.

"Fuck, I didn't protect you."

"It's okay. I'm on birth control. I'm clean."

Stone let out a shaking breath, his dick still twitching deep inside me. "I'm clean too. But hell. I need to do better about taking care of you."

"It's okay. It's okay."

And then I kissed him, falling in love with him all over again.

The boy that I'd loved, the man that I yearned for, and the promise I knew needed to be kept.

He was Stone, he was mine, and I had to hope that in these moments we had for one another—that this couldn't be the end.

CHAPTER FIVE

Stone

THE SUN WARMED my face as I looked up into it and let out a deep breath. It had been a long day on-site, and I was exhausted but still revved. I needed to head home, shower, and then I was going to meet with Sarina. Somehow she had taken me back. It wasn't as if we had forgotten what had happened, but maybe we were just figuring out who we could be now.

I liked working for the Montgomerys. They were good people, took care of their crew, and didn't mind that I couldn't tell them everything.

Maybe it was because I figured a few of them had secrets of their own, or had been through shit the same as I had. But they didn't ask questions. Everything was above board and legal, because hiding from the Kingdom didn't happen. I knew they knew where I was, but they hadn't come for me yet. So that was something I would eventually have to deal with.

The Montgomerys didn't mind that I didn't answer their questions. They appreciated the fact that I did good work and was doing my best to learn.

They did care that I didn't have a truck or vehicle, but between walking, and the city's mass transit, I was making do.

I had never not had a bike or a vehicle. I had always had something. It had been a point of pride for me.

I had left my bike back at the Kingdom, and when I had come here, I had sold the car Arlo had given me, not exactly legal since the car hadn't been in his name either, but it had worked.

The place hadn't asked questions, and I hadn't volunteered anything. I'd gotten the money I needed to get my life started, as well as any money I had on hand, and that was it.

That meant I didn't have a vehicle, I had a shitty apartment, but I was saving.

And, if I was honest, I felt like I was also taking advantage of the fact that Sarina let me stay over.

Her sublet was small but fucking nice.

She had made a life for herself, and I was grateful for that.

If anyone had needed a new way to live, a new focus, it was her.

And she was making it happen.

I was so fucking proud of her.

I knew she was working too hard, and while I was too, I didn't want her to have to.

Maybe I could figure out a way to help her. To make it so she didn't have to work as hard. Not that I figured she'd let me help her. She was so goddamn stubborn, but then again, I wasn't that far off.

That's why I hadn't taken the ride offered when Storm and Wes Montgomery, two of the family members that owned the company, had offered to drive me home. They didn't need to see where I lived, even though they had the address. I didn't need to see the pity on their faces. And frankly, I didn't need the charity. I liked them, but I didn't know them. I needed to do this on my own, even if I might be making a mistake. I had made enough mistakes in the past, didn't want to make any new ones.

I turned the corner, my thoughts on what my next step would be when I heard it.

A single booted foot on gravel, one that shouldn't be there. Because nobody had been following me, I had been alone, and yet the hairs on the back of my neck were rising.

I turned and ducked the fist in the nick of time, but missed the man behind me.

"The King sends his regards," a muffled voice whispered into my ear, and then the fight was on.

Someone grabbed me by the back of my neck and pulled me backward. I stumbled a bit, catching my balance, and stuck my elbow out, hitting the other man in the chest. He moved back, and I punched out, slamming my fist into the mouth of the other man.

It was the Rook and the Knight. They had come for me. They wanted me.

Fuck. I'd been too complacent. No, I hadn't been able to hide entirely, as you couldn't hide from the Kingdom, but they'd still found me. I didn't even have a fucking weapon on me because I didn't want to carry.

But I knew they wouldn't care. I only had my small knife, not even a true weapon, and it wasn't going to be enough. And I couldn't reach it with my hands pinned behind my back, eerily reminiscent of the last time this had happened and I had watched Jeremy die.

Rage filled me at the thought of Sarina being in that position this time instead of Jeremy. I would never forgive myself if she got hurt. I couldn't let them find her. I couldn't lead them to her or have them know that I was close to her again.

I tried to get away but froze as the feel of a blade nicked at my neck.

"I wouldn't move, boy. You never know how clumsy I can be."

"Fuck you," I grumbled, knowing if they were going to do it, they'd have already killed me. They were just waiting. For what, I didn't know, but it had to be something. They wanted me, and now they were going to get me.

I just couldn't let them have Sarina.

"You shouldn't have left. The King wants your head, and he gets what he wants."

"I'm not your fucking pawn. I never have been."

"Really? Because you never moved up in the ranks. Never had enough dick to make it happen."

I snorted. "You don't want to hear about my dick, boy."

"That what you're going to go with? Well, too

bad you're going to die out here all alone. Kind of sad, really. Then again, you always were. Couldn't keep your woman, couldn't keep your friends or family. You already have one foot in the grave, Stone. You shouldn't have run out on the King."

"Fuck. You."

I spat out the words, blood seeping from my cut lip, as the Knight hit me again and again, the Rook holding me back.

I couldn't do much, not with a knife at my throat, but I knew they couldn't kill me, not here out in the open.

At least, that's what I'd hoped.

"What the fuck is going on?" a familiar voice called out from a passing truck. The tires squealed as the brakes slammed, and then the Knight cursed under his breath.

"You're lucky this time, boy," he spat, literally spitting in my face.

I growled, and then the Rook let me go, the knife easily tucked away in his pocket.

They ran, Wes and Storm coming at me. "What the fuck? Stone? Dear God. Come on, let's get you to the hospital."

I shook my head, wiped my mouth with the back

of my hand. "I'm fine. They didn't break anything." I winced, rubbed my side.

"At least they didn't rebreak my ribs."

"Jesus Christ, Stone." Storm shook his head. "You need to see someone."

"I can't. You know why."

They might not know the details, but they knew why. I had kept my secrets on purpose. So I wouldn't go anywhere, but I was damn grateful to see Wes and Storm right now.

"Are they going to come after you again?" Wes asked, his hands on his hips as he glared in the distance.

"I don't know. They should give me space, but hell, I just don't know." I let out a breath, defeat lying heavy on my shoulders. "I won't come back to work. I won't put your family in jeopardy."

Storm frowned. "That's not what we said. We're worried about you."

"What about your family?"

"They didn't jump you on-site. They jumped you around the corner because you're walking home alone. We just won't let that happen again."

"What do you mean? You're going to fight back whoever tries to jump me?"

"No, we'll just make sure you're not alone."

"And for how long?"

"Till they give up? We don't know," Storm growled. "It's not like this is something we're used to, Stone."

"I figured that. You guys shouldn't have to deal with me."

"You shouldn't have to deal with this either. It looks like you're trying to start a new life with your girl out here."

"I'm not a good man, you guys." I swallowed a lump in my throat. "I never have been. Maybe I'm just getting what I deserve."

"Well, that's just a crock of shit," Wes added. "You got out. You do good work here. And while I don't want to hurt anyone, I don't want you to get fucking hurt."

"Well, they found me anyway."

"Did you use your real name on your paperwork?"

I nodded. "They'd have found me no matter what. Might as well not get you guys in trouble."

Wes and Storm met gazes and nodded tightly.

"I know someone that can help," Storm added, and my brows raised.

"Excuse me?"

"He's a friend of the family, at the other part of Montgomery Ink."

"What the hell do you mean?"

"Best not to ask questions. We'll see what we can do to make sure that they know you're off-limits."

"What kind of shit do the Montgomerys get into?" I asked, blinking.

"As I said, don't ask questions." Storm shrugged, and I looked between the twins, wondering what the hell I had gotten into and why I felt oddly safe.

"Now get in the fucking truck, and we'll take you home."

"Can you take me to Sarina's instead?" I asked, my voice low.

"Need to check on her?"

"Yeah. And just, well, you know."

"We do," Wes whispered under his breath, and I got in the back of the truck, wondering how the hell I had met these people and how my life had turned into this.

They dropped me off in front of Sarina's building, and I said my thanks, wondering if I would see them again. They said they had people to help? Maybe. Or maybe I had gotten a concussion, and I was dreaming all of this.

Nobody gave me a second look as I walked up the stairs, and I didn't know what to think about that, but I ignored it. My lip was bloody, I knew I would end up with a black eye, but I didn't look too bad, I figured. I had tried to clean myself up in the truck, but in the end, Sarina would know exactly what had happened.

I should have just gone home. I shouldn't show her this again. What the hell had I been thinking? Maybe I had gotten a concussion.

I turned on my heel to walk out and the door opened and Sarina's voice soothed my soul.

"Stone? What happened?"

I turned, swallowed hard. "I should go home."

"They found you," she whispered, before she tugged on my wrist and pulled me inside. She closed the door behind her, locked the three deadbolts, and put her hands on the door, shaking as she rested her forehead on the metal.

"I shouldn't be here."

"Did they follow you?"

I shook my head, winced. "I don't think so. Wes and Storm scared them off."

Her eyes widened as she looked at me.

"Sarina," I whispered, and swallowed hard.

She moved forward and cupped my cheek, her gaze filling with tears.

"You're hurt. They found you."

"I'm fine. They jumped me, but I'll be more careful next time. Or, I don't know, Sarina. They're always going to be there. There's no hiding."

"I know, I've always been on the lookout, same as Rebel. There's no living your own life if they don't want you to."

She tugged me to the barstool and then pulled out an extensive first aid kit.

"This brings back memories," I said softly.

Her lips quirked into a sad smile. "I know. We've done this before. I did this for my father. My brother. I watched them die, Stone. I watched it all. I don't know if I can do it again."

She reached out, wiped the blood from my lip, and then cursed.

"We can fix it."

"How?"

"I don't know. But I'm not that man anymore. You're not that girl. We'll find a way out. We're already halfway there."

"Halfway there, and yet it seems like we have so much further to go. I can't watch you die, Stone. I can't have our past come back."

I tugged on her arm and pulled her close to me, holding her as tightly as I could without hurting either one of us. "I don't know what I'm going to do, what we can do. I'm never going to let them hurt you."

"What if we don't have a choice, Stone?"

I swallowed hard, but I didn't answer. Because I would die before I let them hurt her, or I would kill anybody who got too close.

What was another mark on my soul, after all?

CHAPTER SIX

Sarina

MY HANDS KEPT SHAKING as I made coffee. That wasn't the best thing for someone who worked at a café as a barista. But I needed to focus. I needed to work, make money, and maybe find a way for Stone and me to leave again.

It was so odd to think how quickly the two of us had become a pair again. As if no time at all had passed between us, and yet all the time had passed.

I let out a deep breath, opened and closed my hands, and did my best to focus.

Hailey was next door with her husband, delivering drinks to the tattoo artists while I was left operating the espresso maker, working on a latte for an order. The rest of the staff was friendly, welcoming and didn't ask too many prying questions. I had always found that slightly odd since they tended to ask and pry with everyone else. But maybe it was because they knew I couldn't answer. Or at least give the answers that they wanted.

The Kingdom was watching. In the back of my mind, I had always known that. It was why I took the precautions that I could and why I always felt as if I needed to be two steps ahead. The fact that the Rook and the Knight had been here, had come all the way from Desolation, New York, worried me. I didn't know if they had truly gone back. What if they hadn't? What if they were waiting for us to make a mistake again?

I didn't know what I would do if I lost Stone. Or if I lost myself.

I had been honest with Stone before. Falling into a relationship might have been the worst mistake of my life, but walking away from him hurt just as much. Because I loved him. I loved who he was and how he made me feel.

So somehow, not being able to find a future, or at least look into seeing who we could be, pained me.

This wasn't what I had signed up for. This wasn't what I thought I could be, but now here we were, there was no going back. I had taken Stone into my bed and had brought him into my heart long before he had come to Denver to find me.

"Are you okay?" Hailey asked as she moved forward, her hand on my wrist.

I looked up at her and blinked, and gave her a watery smile. "I think I didn't get enough sleep."

She met my gaze, and I wasn't sure she believed me. It was the truth, but not why I felt like this.

"Okay, well, if you need anything, you let me know. I'm here."

I swallowed hard. "Thanks for everything."

"Why does that sound like a goodbye?" Hailey asked, her voice soft.

"It's not."

I swallowed hard. At least, I don't think so.

"Your shift was over twenty minutes ago, Sarina. Why don't you head home? Take the afternoon off from the bar."

I shook my head. "That would be nice, but I don't have the option of doing that."

"No, I don't think you do. You work so hard, Sarina. But I hope you know we think of you like family here. You and Stone."

I frowned. "Really?"

"Of course. Stone works for the other Montgomerys, just like we're family with these Montgomerys. I know this is probably invasive even to mention, but I heard about what happened."

I froze. "What did you hear?"

Hailey winced, and it was such an odd expression on a beautiful face. "I heard that Stone was hurt. That Wes and Storm found him. I'm glad that they found him. And while I don't know all the details, my husband said that things are being taken care of."

I shook my head. "I can't talk about it, Hailey."

"I know. I just want you to know that we love you, and we're here for you. Don't run, okay? We'll help keep you safe."

I met her gaze. "I don't think you know who you'd be fighting to try to keep me safe."

"No, I don't. It's completely out of my wheelhouse. I'm here if you need me. And if you do need to go, know that you can always come back. This will always be your home."

She squeezed my hands and then she walked away. I sighed, knowing I needed to leave. Maybe I needed to leave town. It might be safer for those that I had come to care for. But where would Stone and I go? And would I even go with him?

He had been back for two months, we had been together for only a month of that time, and he had already been hurt.

The Kingdom had already come to Denver after so long of leaving me alone.

Was it because Stone was the last straw? Or had they just been waiting until I had been lulled into complacency?

I wasn't sure, but I needed to make a decision.

I grabbed my bag and walked out of the back alley, heading towards Ink on Tap. My senses were on alert since I was afraid that *he* would find me any moment. The King hadn't wanted me in ages. Maybe this wasn't about me. Maybe it was because Stone had left without permission. Hopefully, the King would forget Stone eventually, and someone else would make a mistake. Or another club or group would anger him, and he'd focus all of his attentions on them. That was what had happened with me, and it had given me over four years of relative peace. I might have been constantly on edge, but that was the path I had been set on from birth. The path I couldn't walk away from.

"Sarina?"

I turned, my hands outstretched, my taser in my right hand, and I looked up at Stone.

He held both hands up and cursed under his breath. "Fuck. Sorry, the bus was late, and I came here to walk you to the bar."

Relief speared through me, and I threw my arms around him, careful not to accidentally tackle him. "You scared the crap out of me."

"I can see that. I'm glad you have your taser."

"Who knows if it'll ever be enough," I whispered, and I kissed him softly.

"I hate that you're so on edge, that you're so afraid."

I shook my head. "You're in the same boat."

"Maybe. You were safe before I came here."

"Was I? Or was I just led to believe that?"

"I don't know, baby. Let's get you to work. Maybe Rebel will hire me too." He winked at me, and I grinned.

"He's always looking for a bouncer. It is a gay bar."

"Hey, I'll have you know I will protect anybody in that bar. As long as you're safe."

"I missed you," I whispered as I leaned into him.

"I missed you, too."

And I knew we both weren't talking about the afternoon and morning that we hadn't seen each other. No, it had been a long four years, four years in which we'd had to stay apart to keep each other safe, and it had taken me a while to realize exactly why.

We turned the corner, and Stone let out a shout. I hit the ground as he pushed me down, covering my body. Gunshots rained above us, and I screamed, trying to cover Stone as well, but there was no use, nowhere to hide.

We were slightly behind a dumpster, but it wasn't enough.

"As I said, the King wants you back. You don't get to decide to leave."

Stone growled, pulled me back from the ground, and I ignored the sting in my palms from where I had hit the gravel and now bled.

"Stay here."

"No," I shouted, my throat tight. I gripped his wrist. "Don't go."

Stay safe.

"They're going to kill you."

"No, they're going to kill you," I spat.

And then we were surrounded. They had guns, knives, and they came at us.

"You really shouldn't have left. And to think, you had had everything. A home, food in your belly, protection. And then you left." The Knight looked over Stone's shoulder. "Left to find her. The little bitch the King doesn't even want anymore."

I should have felt relief at that, but I couldn't, not when this could be the end.

The Knight came forward, glaring at Stone.

"You always were a little bitch, just like her."

I moved without thinking, aware that only the Knight had a gun in his hand. Everyone else seemed to just have knives. Not that there was anything *just* about that.

I moved forward, my taser out, and I got him in the belly. The Knight let out a shocked scream and hit the ground.

Stone cursed under his breath, pulled me back, and kicked the gun underneath the dumpster.

"Run," he yelled at me as the others moved forward, shock in their gazes that I would be the one to do that.

The Rook came at us, knife out, and Stone moved quickly, faster than I had ever seen him move before. He gripped the Rook's wrist, twisted. The other man let out a shout. The knife fell to the ground with a clang, and then Stone punched him hard in the face.

Another man came at us, and I kicked out, using

the training that I had had from self-defense, and kicked the other man in the balls.

I tugged at Stone, knowing we needed to get away, but there were too many of them.

They couldn't get the gun, but they had knives, and I wasn't sure a taser was going to be able to get all of them.

I looked at Stone, so afraid I had made the wrong choice, that he would die and it was going to be my fault.

The Rook came at us again, the Knight still twitching on the ground, and then the most sacred sound in the world came.

Sirens hit my ears, and Stone and I froze, hands up in the air as the police came, then their words shouting at us to freeze, to not move. The alley filled with the authorities, and Stone and I went to our knees, trying to explain what happened.

Considering the way that it looked and the fact that Rebel and Hailey came out, her husband and the other tattoo artists with her to give their explanations as well, I knew that we would be okay.

The King was going to lose some of his inner circle, at least for the moment, but we weren't going to die right then.

Somehow.

I looked at Stone, my eyes wide, and prayed that this could be the end. Or at least an end.

It would be too much trouble. That anyone the King sent from the Ruin towards us would be sent right back, worse off. That Stone was out.

That I was out.

My father had lied. And then he had died. My brother had done much the same.

Stone was here. And he had protected me, and he had let me protect him.

I had to hope that this would be it. That this could be the start of our future.

The sounds of bullets, of shouts, of screams would echo in my mind until the end of my days, but maybe this could be the end. Or an end.

And finally, a beginning.

CHAPTER SEVEN

Stone

I'D GOTTEN my first tattoo when I was fifteen years old. My father had sat me down, and the Kingdom's artist had branded me. I wore their ink on my flesh and their scars on my memories. But not my soul anymore.

I wasn't that man anymore.

It had been a year since the cops had come. Since everything had changed.

The Kingdom hadn't sent another man. We hadn't even heard from them. The Knight was still in jail, the Rook having gotten out on a technicality, but he hadn't come by either. Last I had heard, the King had sent him off, exiled him for failing to get me. For failing to get Sarina.

In the end, it didn't matter because they wouldn't be coming for us anymore.

I had gotten a few more tattoos since, mostly all of them thanks to the Kingdom itself. You wore your ink on your body to prove who you were to those in charge, and I wasn't with them anymore.

The only tattoo I'd ever gotten for myself was a small S hidden among my sleeve.

An S for Sarina, though some had thought it was for me.

I hadn't begrudged them on that or made them think anything different.

Now this ink was for me.

I let out a deep breath, letting the Montgomery behind me have as much space to work with as possible. We were covering up the brands that were from the Kingdom that had nothing to do with my present or my future.

Doing coverups were a lot more fucking painful than the tattoos to begin with, but I didn't mind. If this were my penance to pay for the mistakes I had made in the past, I would freely pay them.

Sarina sat in the next booth over, a woman with

dark hair with pink streaks bent over and working on her back. Sarina was getting ink for herself, not a coverup, like me. She could focus on her future ink and paths, while I still had a long way to go working my way through my sins.

We were making this work for the two of us. Though I wasn't sure what would happen next, we would find a way to make all of this work. We were already well on our way to doing so.

We weren't the people we had been years ago. And for that, I was grateful.

I had been young, rash, and stupid the first time I had been with Sarina.

Now I was making choices for myself, and we were finding our path together.

She wore my ring on her finger and would soon carry my name as well.

She grinned up at me, and I smiled back, ignoring the pain as Austin went over the mark, again and again, doing his best to cover up the sins of my past.

I had fallen in love with Sarina long before I realized what love was.

She had been my salvation, my path, my future.

And now she was the promise I had never meant to make, the promise I had thought a dream.

The Kingdom was long gone. We were never going back.

In the end, however, she was my empress, my queen, my everything.

And I was one lucky son of a bitch.

****

Want more of Carrie Ann's romances?
Try Inked Persuasion

A NOTE FROM CARRIE ANN RYAN

Thank you so much for reading **INKED KINGDOM!**

I loved writing this little romance that was so unlike my normal books! When the authors of Underworld Kings asked me to join them for a special project, I couldn't say no!

You can find more stand alone romance set in the world of the Ruin and the UNDERWORLD KINGS, as well as a few familiar Montgomerys in my Montgomery Ink series!

The Montgomery Ink: Fort Collins Series:

Book 1: Inked Persuasion

Book 2: Inked Obsession

Book 3: Inked Devotion

Book 3.5: Nothing But Ink

Book 4: Inked Craving

Book 5: Inked Temptation

If you want to make sure you know what's coming next from me, you can sign up for my newsletter at www.CarrieAnnRyan.com; follow me on twitter at @CarrieAnnRyan, or like my Facebook page. I also have a Facebook Fan Club where we have trivia, chats, and other goodies. You guys are the reason I get to do what I do and I thank you.

Make sure you're signed up for my MAILING LIST so you can know when the next releases are available as well as find giveaways and FREE READS.

Happy Reading!

Want to keep up to date with the next Carrie Ann Ryan Release? Receive Text Alerts easily!

Text CARRIE to 210-741-8720

ABOUT THE AUTHOR

Carrie Ann Ryan is the New York Times and USA Today bestselling author of contemporary, paranormal, and young adult romance. Her works include the Montgomery Ink, Redwood Pack, Fractured Connections, and Elements of Five series, which have sold over 3.0 million books worldwide. She started writing while in graduate school for her advanced degree in chemistry and hasn't stopped since. Carrie Ann has written over seventy-five novels and novellas with more in the works. When she's not losing herself in her emotional and action-packed worlds, she's reading as much as she can while wrangling her clowder of cats who have more followers than she does.

www.CarrieAnnRyan.com

ALSO FROM CARRIE ANN RYAN

The Montgomery Ink: Fort Collins Series:

Book 1: Inked Persuasion

Book 2: Inked Obsession

Book 3: Inked Devotion

Book 3.5: Nothing But Ink

Book 4: Inked Craving

Book 5: Inked Temptation

The On My Own Series:

Book 1: My One Night

Book 2: My Rebound

Book 3: My Next Play

Book 4: My Bad Decisions

The Ravenwood Coven Series:

Book 1: Dawn Unearthed

Book 2: Dusk Unveiled

Book 3: Evernight Unleashed

Montgomery Ink:

Book 0.5: Ink Inspired

Book 0.6: Ink Reunited

Book 1: Delicate Ink

Book 1.5: Forever Ink

Book 2: Tempting Boundaries

Book 3: Harder than Words

Book 3.5: Finally Found You

Book 4: Written in Ink

Book 4.5: Hidden Ink

Book 5: Ink Enduring

Book 6: Ink Exposed

Book 6.5: Adoring Ink

Book 6.6: Love, Honor, & Ink

Book 7: Inked Expressions

Book 7.3: Dropout

Book 7.5: Executive Ink

Book 8: Inked Memories

Book 8.5: Inked Nights

Book 8.7: Second Chance Ink

Montgomery Ink: Colorado Springs

Book 1: Fallen Ink

Book 2: Restless Ink

Book 2.5: Ashes to Ink

Book 3: Jagged Ink

Book 3.5: Ink by Numbers

The Montgomery Ink: Boulder Series:

Book 1: Wrapped in Ink

Book 2: Sated in Ink

Book 3: Embraced in Ink

Book 4: Seduced in Ink

Book 4.5: Captured in Ink

The Gallagher Brothers Series:

Book 1: Love Restored

Book 2: Passion Restored

Book 3: Hope Restored

The Whiskey and Lies Series:

Book 1: Whiskey Secrets

Book 2: Whiskey Reveals

Book 3: Whiskey Undone

The Fractured Connections Series:

Book 1: Breaking Without You

Book 2: Shouldn't Have You

Book 3: Falling With You

Book 4: Taken With You

The Less Than Series:

Book 1: Breathless With Her

Book 2: Reckless With You

Book 3: Shameless With Him

The Promise Me Series:

Book 1: Forever Only Once

Book 2: From That Moment

Book 3: Far From Destined

Book 4: From Our First

Redwood Pack Series:

Book 1: An Alpha's Path

Book 2: A Taste for a Mate

Book 3: Trinity Bound

Book 3.5: A Night Away

Book 4: Enforcer's Redemption

Book 4.5: Blurred Expectations

Book 4.7: Forgiveness

Book 5: Shattered Emotions

Book 6: Hidden Destiny

Book 6.5: A Beta's Haven

Book 7: Fighting Fate

Book 7.5: Loving the Omega

Book 7.7: The Hunted Heart

Book 8: Wicked Wolf

The Talon Pack:

Book 1: Tattered Loyalties

Book 2: An Alpha's Choice

Book 3: Mated in Mist

Book 4: Wolf Betrayed

Book 5: Fractured Silence

Book 6: Destiny Disgraced

Book 7: Eternal Mourning

Book 8: Strength Enduring

Book 9: Forever Broken

The Elements of Five Series:

Book 1: From Breath and Ruin

Book 2: From Flame and Ash

Book 3: From Spirit and Binding

Book 4: From Shadow and Silence

The Branded Pack Series:
(Written with Alexandra Ivy)

Book 1: Stolen and Forgiven

Book 2: Abandoned and Unseen

Book 3: Buried and Shadowed

Dante's Circle Series:

Book 1: Dust of My Wings

Book 2: Her Warriors' Three Wishes

Book 3: An Unlucky Moon

Book 3.5: His Choice

Book 4: Tangled Innocence

Book 5: Fierce Enchantment

Book 6: An Immortal's Song

Book 7: Prowled Darkness

Book 8: Dante's Circle Reborn

Holiday, Montana Series:

Book 1: Charmed Spirits

Book 2: Santa's Executive

Book 3: Finding Abigail

Book 4: Her Lucky Love

Book 5: Dreams of Ivory

The Tattered Royals Series:

Book 1: Royal Line

Book 2: Enemy Heir

The Happy Ever After Series:

Flame and Ink

Ink Ever After

INKED PERSUASION

Annabelle

I WAS GOING to shake my hips, dance, and drink the night away. Okay, perhaps not the last thing, but I would drink a little.

I grinned over at my sister, Paige, who smiled widely back. I gave her a little wave. She leaned into her new boyfriend, Colton, joy evident in her expression. I didn't know this Colton, but he was brave for coming to a Montgomery event so fresh into their relationship. Even at a bar on a weekend night—seemingly an innocent time. But when it came to the

Montgomerys and how we circled our prey, no time was innocent.

"You are staring at Paige like you are ready to grill her new boyfriend."

I looked up at my big brother, Beckett, and smiled. "Maybe I am. After all, this is the first time she's brought him to a family event. It's a big thing."

Beckett shook his head and pushed his dark hair away from his face. He needed a haircut, so did his twin, Benjamin, but the two of them seemed to be going for a mountain man look. Soon, their beards would be annoyingly bushy, rather than what was on-trend these days. Of course, we were in Fort Collins, Colorado, not in Boulder or down in Denver with some of the other Montgomery cousins. We had standards when it came to facial hair. Not that I actually believed that, but I knew some of our friends did.

"Now you're grinning. Are you thinking of something evil?" Beckett asked.

I leaned my head on his shoulder and sighed. "Just thinking about the cousins."

"Which ones?" He sounded a little nervous, and I frowned, looking up at him. "We like all of our cousins. I can't even say *most* because we *actually* do like them all. What's with the tone?"

He shook his head, wrapped his arm around my shoulders, and pulled me closer to him. He smelled like sandalwood and soap. He must have showered before he came out to join us at Riggs'. He had been out on the grounds all day, all of us working hard to finish up the last bit of the leading project before we started on the new, larger one that had also been keeping me up at night.

"Dad was grumbling about something the other Montgomerys did, and I'm not in the mood to talk about it. We are here to drink, have fun, and grill not only this new Colton but our baby brother's new beau, as well."

"Did you say 'beau?'" Benjamin asked, frowning as he walked toward us. Beckett flipped him off.

Benjamin was the mirror image of Beckett. Why my parents decided to give both sets of twins similar names, I would never know.

Beckett and Benjamin had been born first, and then Archer and I came next. If anything, they should have given the older brothers names starting with A, and then Archer and I should have gotten B names. But wanting to go alphabetical had not been in the cards, apparently.

Our baby sister Paige was the only one of us without a twin. And, sadly, she did not have a name that started with a C, much to her consternation. She'd even tried to go as a Chloe or Christine for a while when we were younger, but she always ended up as Paige.

When Beckett and I didn't answer him in time, Benjamin cleared his throat. "What are you guys talking about?"

Beckett shrugged. "Nothing, just Dad being a jerk. And now I am getting ready to be by Annabelle's side when we grill the two new people who've joined us tonight."

Benjamin shook his head and raised his brow at his older brother. "You know, you said the word *beau*, and that's not a word I think has ever left your mouth before."

Beckett's lips twitched, and I grinned. The two of them usually took turns being the broodiest. Generally, they had scowls under those beards and rarely smiled or laughed. I wasn't sure why they were always so serious. Maybe they'd been a little less severe as babies. And then Archer and I had shown up and probably terrorized the twins. I might not be as wild as Archer, or as carefree—I couldn't be, not after everything that had happened—but I still smiled a lot more than Benjamin and Beckett did.

Paige was a unique delight. Which was exactly how she liked and wanted it, even if she *had* said at one point that she wished she had a twin. She was the brightest one of us all, the happiest, and the sweetest. At least that's what I thought. Paige called me sweet, though usually when she was making fun of me for being weird. Because I *was* weird. I couldn't help it. I was a Montgomery.

"Okay, there's Archer and his boyfriend, Marc. Now we have the two youngest and their new *beaus*," Benjamin said, and Beckett flipped him off again.

"We're not actually going to terrorize them, are we?" I asked. "Because I kind of want our siblings to be happy."

Beckett raised a brow and shook his head. "Oh, they can be happy—once they pass our test."

"We're still learning how to do this whole big brother and sister thing when it comes to our siblings' relationships," Beckett explained and then held up three fingers, getting the bartender's attention. Riggs gave Benjamin a wink before pouring three shots of tequila.

I shook my head. "I swear, everywhere you go, everyone loves you."

Benjamin didn't smile, but he did snort. "No, that would be Archer. I just learned how to give that come-hither look to bartenders from our baby brother."

Beckett and I burst out laughing.

"And if you ever tell anyone I said that, I will hunt you down," Benjamin warned.

I shook my head, picked up my shot, and downed it. I closed my eyes and winced but didn't reach for salt or lime. Doing a tequila shot with the type of tequila Benjamin liked did not usually require salt or lime. And the twins would make fun of me if I asked for them. Of course, it was all out of love. But still, I wasn't about to open myself for teasing.

I looked across the crowd at the bar to our two siblings and their significant others. "I think we should start with Paige and Colton. They seem to be more serious."

Beckett nodded. "I agree. They've also had at least three weeks longer than Archer and Marc."

Benjamin sighed. "I swear we should have started taking notes or something so we knew exactly how to interrogate them to make sure they're good enough for our baby siblings."

I smiled and listened as my brothers went through their plans. I might be Archer's twin, but I always felt a little more protective of him, a little older than the five minutes that separated us. Though he likely thought the same of me.

"You think that's too much?" Benjamin asked, frowning.

Beckett shook his head. "No, we need to get this right. After all, we've never had to deal with serious relationships before. While the rest of the Montgomerys got married, we've all stayed single. We need to get ready for the first marriage, you know?"

Both of the twins froze and risked glances at me.

I gave them a soft smile and shook my head. "Exactly," I said, not daring to broach that subject. "We need to get ready and interrogate these two new people who dared to step out with our siblings."

"Okay, now I'm a little afraid of what you guys are talking about," my twin said as he came towards us. He leaned down and kissed my cheek, his hand holding Marc's.

Archer looked like a slightly smaller version of Beckett and Benjamin. He wasn't as wide, and he didn't have a beard at the moment. But he had the same startling blue eyes and wicked grin. Not that the older twins showed those grins often, but when they did, they looked just like Archer.

I looked like him, too—after all, we were twins.

But I was a little softer around the edges, though my jaw was slightly more pointed than Paige's. We all looked like Montgomerys—both sides of the family.

My mother's maiden name was also Montgomery. She was the youngest sister of the Colorado Montgomerys, a completely different line than my father's. It made things a little weird for my dad. But having those connections meant we had dozens of cousins around the country, even more than *my* cousins, who lived close by.

"I feel like I should be scared," Marc said, grinning.

He was blond-haired, brown-eyed, and beautiful. *Shockingly* beautiful if I were honest. He was slender, wore well-cut pants, and a button-up shirt tucked in. At some point, he had rolled up his sleeves so his forearms showed, and I noticed he had a small tattoo peeking out. I wondered if one of our cousins had inked him, even though it was a vast country and world, and anybody could have done it. Still, I liked the idea that a Montgomery may have inked his skin.

"You should be scared," I said, leaning forward as Marc kissed my other cheek.

"I'll try to be. However, I think I overheard that you're going to take care of Paige's new guy first.

This is great. I can watch how it happens and study the dynamics." Marc grinned, then wrapped his arm around Archer's waist. My twin beamed.

I loved that it looked as if Archer were falling in love. He appeared so happy. And if Marc hurt him, I would find a way to make the man scream in pain and agony while the other siblings took care of him.

Because nobody hurt my twin.

"You're looking a little vicious over there," Archer whispered, and I grimaced.

"Sorry, just thinking of weird things. And, Marc? You should still be wary. Because while we may practice certain techniques on Paige's new guy, you have your own set of rules."

Beckett nodded. "She's right. We have lists."

Benjamin nodded, his gaze on Marc, and Marc looked between all of us before he rocked back on his heels.

"You guys are a little scary when you're all together."

I looked at my brothers, and we all burst out laughing. "We're not that bad. I promise."

"They will not be that bad," Archer warned, and I didn't know if the warning was for Marc or us.

Finally, Paige tugged her boyfriend off the dance

floor and skipped over to us, the smile on her face radiant. "Well, hello. Are you all talking about how you're going to maim and torture poor Colton and Marc for daring to come near your baby siblings?" she asked in a singsong. She leaned into Colton, and the big redheaded man rolled his eyes.

"You need to let them think they're all secretive with their glowering, darling," Colton said, kissing the top of her head.

"Oops," Paige said, giggling.

Everybody looked so damn happy, and I couldn't help but be content as well. I might not have the same type of connections they did with another human being right now, but I didn't need that. I'd nearly had a chance before, and I wasn't about to do that again. However, I could still have fun. And we were all happy, healthy, and here.

That was all that mattered.

"Okay, one more shot as a family, and then I'm dancing."

"That sounds like a plan," Archer said before meeting the bartender's gaze over my head.

I resisted the urge to roll my eyes as Archer gave that same look Benjamin had stolen. Riggs poured a round of shots for everybody, and immediately after, the family was on the dance floor.

My brothers did their best to block me in, stopping anybody from daring to come near. I slowly moved away, rolling my eyes.

"You know, if you keep letting them pin you in, you'll never get to dance with a guy," Paige said, taking my hand. "What about the bartender? Riggs?" She gestured over to the man with his honey eyes and wicked grin.

"I'm pretty sure he only has eyes for Benjamin. And maybe Archer. Not so much for me."

"His eyes were on your butt. I'm pretty sure he swings for any Montgomery," Paige corrected.

"Well, my gaze doesn't swing that way—at least not tonight. I want to have fun and not deal with men or egos or penises or anything of the sort."

Colton's eyes widened as he came up from behind Paige and slowly raised his hands before backing away.

I winced. "You are going to have to explain to Colton that I didn't mean to just blurt out the word *penis* like that." I blinked. "Or now. Again."

Paige put her hand over her mouth, her eyes wide. "Annabelle," she mock-whispered.

"I'm sorry. Go. Fix it. I'm not crazy. I promise."

"You know, that's what they all say," Paige said

solemnly before grinning again. She kissed my cheek and moved off to her boyfriend.

I danced with two of my brothers and then between another group of women who had come in for a good night. I felt free. I might not have a boyfriend or anybody on the horizon, but that was fine. Honestly, I didn't need that in my life. I had my family, a job I loved, and a massive project coming up that I needed to focus on.

I didn't need any more complications.

By the time the night wound down, my feet ached, and I regretted my shoes. But they made my butt look great, and I felt sexy in them. Sometimes, a girl just needed to feel good. I sat in the passenger seat as Benjamin drove me home. He'd only had one drink for the night, and I'd had three. It only made sense.

"Thanks for being the DD tonight," I said softly.

"Thank you for not taking off your shoes in my car because I know you want to," he said wryly. "You know I hate feet."

He didn't, but he liked making fun of me. I stuck out my tongue at him. "Weirdo," I teased.

"Maybe. But as I'm the one who is driving, and it's my car, you get to follow my rules. And I'll do you the courtesy of not taking off my shoes in your car when *my* feet hurt."

I grinned and shook my head. We pulled into my driveway, and Benjamin looked over at the house to my right. "Looks like your new neighbor moved in."

I nodded. "These houses get gobbled up fast, even in this housing market."

"It's a boom right now, hence why I have a job," my brother, the landscape architect, said. "But I'm sad your previous neighbor had to move away."

"Me, too. I liked her. Hopefully, this new person is just as quiet, doesn't have forty kids that will be in my yard, and is a happy person."

"You know we're going to end up becoming those crotchety old people who hold brooms and tell kids to get off their lawns."

"Well, if they would stop playing in my yard and play in theirs, it wouldn't be a problem," I said, laughing.

"You're talking to a man who works on land-scapes for a living, I understand." He kissed the top of my head before I got out of the car.

"Thank you," I said.

"Be careful," Benjamin added, and I resisted the urge to roll my eyes.

My brothers acted like I could be snatched off the street in front of my home while they watched. But I was careful. I put my key in the lock, walked inside, and then turned and waved as Benjamin drove off. I let out a breath and then frowned as I looked over at the phonebook on my driveway. I hadn't noticed it being delivered earlier, and I didn't want it outside all night. I sighed and went to pick it up.

"Hey."

I whirled, dropped my keys, and tripped over my heels. I fell on my ass, the pavement digging into my palms. I looked up at the man silhouetted against the moonlight.

"Crap. I'm sorry. I didn't mean to startle you or freak you out. I was just letting you know that I was out here, headed into my house. But I accidentally scared you anyway." He held up a hand, and I looked at him, not wanting to go near him. "Seriously, let me help you up. I promise I'll stand here, and you can go back inside. Only wanted to say hello. I'm your new neighbor."

I frowned, feeling like I knew that voice, but I didn't know from where. Or how.

He could be a serial killer. If I kept sitting there,

he could still try to kill me. I knew I should at least act like I knew what I was doing and not appear scared. I'd probably be able to fight him off better if I were standing. Maybe. I slid my hand into his and let him help me up. I dusted off my butt and then moved back a few steps, needing space.

My heart thudded, and my ankle hurt more as if I had twisted it.

"I am sorry," the man repeated. "Anyway, as I said, I'm your new neighbor. Jacob. Jacob Queen."

Ice slid over me as he stepped into the beam from my porch light. I did the same, my past coming at me full force. I swallowed hard, trying to catch my breath.

No, it couldn't be this. Not in the house I had built. Not in my family's neighborhood, the one we'd put our blood, sweat, and tears into.

This couldn't be Jacob. He couldn't be back.

But as he looked at me, his face suddenly devoid of color, I knew he recognized me. I knew this was the same Jacob.

"You," he whispered.

"You," I echoed.

And then he glowered at me, turned on his heel, and stomped away.

I couldn't help but look at the back of the man who had grown up with my late husband. His brother. And the one man in the whole world I knew hated me more with each and every breath.

Want more of Carrie Ann's romances?
Try Inked Persuasion

Made in the USA
Coppell, TX
24 October 2021

64609536R00066